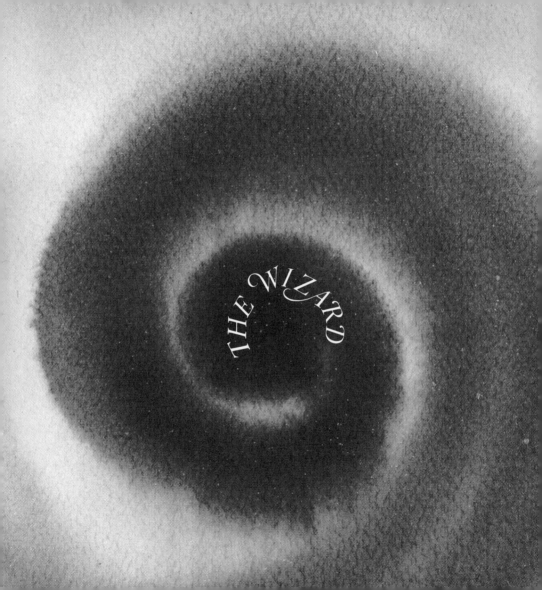

THE WIZARD

The

WIZARD

BY Bill Martin JR.

With Pictures by SAL MURDOCCA

ISBN: 0-03-084583-1

HOLT, RINEHART AND WINSTON, INC.
New York, Toronto, London, Sydney

I dance.

I sing.

I run.

I wing.

I skip.

I jump.

I hop.

I hump.

I twist.

I twirl.

I wheel.

I whirl.

I squat.

I kneel.

I sit.

I heel.

I take off.

I fly.

I low.

I high.

I soar.

I roll.

I dive.

I swoll.

I loop the loop.

I hoop the hoop.

I parachute.

wh ooooooooooooooo oops!

I disappear.

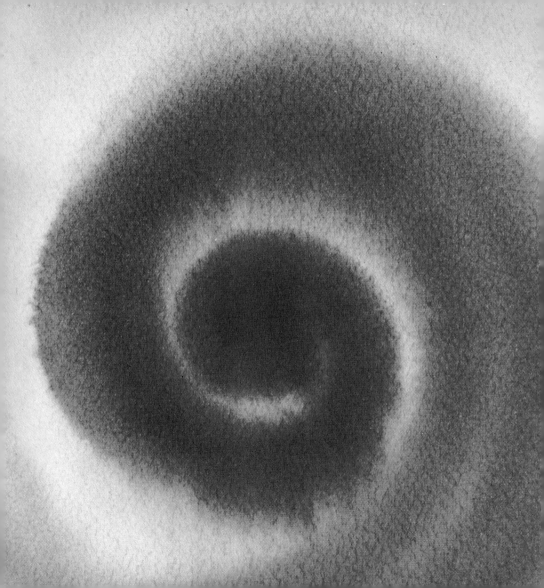